The Gift of the Magi

for
Rod &
Jody
—J.W.

Published by Ideals Publishing Corporation
Nashville, Tennessee
ISBN 0-8249-8388-2

The Gift of the Magi

O. Henry
Illustrated by Jody Wheeler

IDEALS CHILDREN'S BOOKS
Nashville, Tennessee

One dollar and eighty-seven cents. That was all. And sixty cents was in pennies—pennies saved one and two at a time by bargaining with the grocer and the vegetable man and the butcher. Three times Della counted it. One dollar and eighty-seven cents. And the next day would be Christmas.

There was clearly nothing to do but flop down on the shabby little couch and cry. So that's what Della did.

The home in which Della lay was a furnished apartment which rented for $8.00 per week. Yes, furnished—but rather poorly so.

In the hallway below was a mailbox into which no letter would go and an electric doorbell from which no sound would ever be heard.

On the mailbox was a card bearing the name ''Mr. James Dillingham Young.'' But whenever Mr. James Dillingham Young came home and reached his apartment above, he was called ''Jim'' and greatly hugged by Mrs. James Dillingham Young, already introduced to you as Della.

Della finished her crying, wiped her eyes, and powdered her face. She stood by the window and looked out dully at a gray cat walking a gray fence in a gray backyard. The next day would be Christmas Day, and she had only $1.87 with which to buy Jim a present. She had been saving every penny she could for months, but Jim's salary of twenty dollars a week didn't go far. And expenses had been greater than she expected. And now Della had only $1.87 to buy a present for Jim.

There was a mirror made of strips of glass in the apartment. With a little moving about, Della could see a fairly accurate picture of her looks. She suddenly whirled from the window and stood before the mirror.

Her eyes were shining brilliantly, but her face had lost its color within twenty seconds. Rapidly she pulled down her hair and let it fall to its full length.

Now, there were two possessions of the James Dillingham Youngs in which they both took great pride. One was Jim's gold watch that had been his father's and his grandfather's. The other was Della's long hair.

So now Della's beautiful hair fell about her, rippling and shining like a cascade of brown waters. It reached below her knee and almost to her ankle. She did it up again quickly, pausing only once as a tear or two splashed on the worn red carpet.

On went her old brown jacket; on went her old brown hat.

With a whirl of skirts and with the brilliant sparkle still in her eyes, she fluttered out the door and down the stairs to the street.

Della ran down the street, and where she stopped, the sign read: "Mme. Sofronie. Hair Goods of All Kinds."

One flight up Della ran and then collected herself, panting.

"Will you buy my hair?" asked Della.

"I buy hair," said Madame. "Take your hat off and let's have a look at it."

Down rippled the brown cascade.

"Twenty dollars," said Madame, lifting the mass of hair with a practiced hand.

"Give me the money, quickly," said Della.

The next two hours flew by as Della searched through the stores looking for Jim's present.

She found it at last. It surely had been made for Jim and no one else. There was no other like it in any of the stores, and she had turned all of them inside out. It was a platinum watch chain, simple, yet elegant, in design.

As soon as she saw it, Della knew that it must be Jim's. The chain was like him. Quietness and value— the description applied to both. Twenty-one dollars they took from her for it, and she hurried home with the eighty-seven cents that was left.

Grand as the watch was, Jim now sometimes looked at it secretly because he was ashamed of the old leather strap that he used in place of a chain. With that chain on his watch, Jim could be proud to check the time in any company.

When Della reached home, her excitement gave way to reason. She got out her curling irons and went to work on her hair, repairing the damage done by cutting it to buy Jim's present. But her love for Jim was stronger than her love for her hair.

Within forty minutes her head was covered with tiny, close-lying curls. She looked at her reflection in the mirror long and hard.

"If Jim doesn't kill me," she said to herself, "before he takes a second look at me, he'll say I look like a Coney Island chorus girl. But what could I do—oh! what could I do with a dollar and eighty-seven cents?"

At seven o'clock the coffee was made and the frying pan was on the back of the stove, hot and ready to cook the chops.

Jim was never late, so Della doubled the watch chain in her hand and sat on the corner of the table near the door that he always entered. Then she heard his step on the stair, and she turned pale for just a moment. She had a habit of saying little quiet prayers about the simplest everyday things, and now she whispered, "Please, God, make him think I am still pretty."

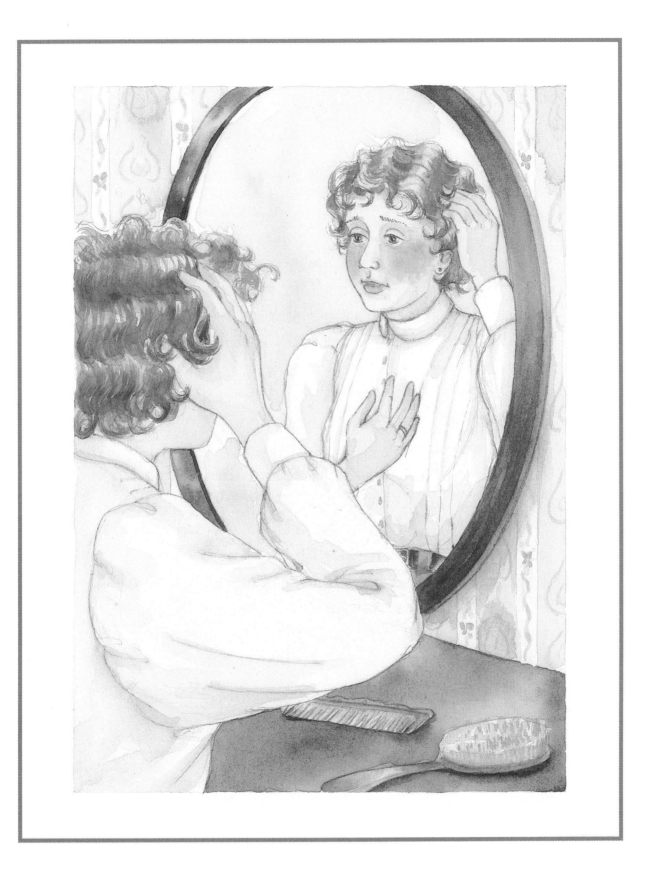

The door opened and Jim stepped in and closed it. He looked thin and very serious. Poor fellow, he needed a new overcoat and he was without gloves.

Jim stopped inside the door and stood still, staring at Della. There was an expression in his eyes that she could not read, and it terrified her. It was not anger, nor surprise, nor disapproval, nor horror, nor any of the sentiments that she had been prepared for.

He simply stared at her with that peculiar expression on his face.

Della wriggled off the table and went toward him.

"Jim, darling," she cried, "don't look at me that way. I had my hair cut off and sold it because I couldn't have lived through Christmas without giving you a present. It'll grow out again—you won't mind, will you? I just had to do it. My hair grows awfully fast. Say 'Merry Christmas!' Jim, and let's be happy. You don't know what a nice, what a beautiful, wonderful gift I've got for you."

"You've cut off your hair?" asked Jim, as if he couldn't quite believe what he was seeing.

"Cut it off and sold it," said Della. "Don't you like me just as well, anyhow? I'm me without my hair, aren't I?"

Jim looked about the room curiously.

"You say your hair is gone?" he said with an air almost of stupidity.

"You needn't look for it," said Della. "It's sold, I tell you—sold and gone too. It's Christmas Eve, boy. Be good to me, for it went for you. Maybe the hairs of my head were numbered," she went on with a sudden serious sweetness, "but nobody could ever count my love for you.

"Shall I put the chops on, Jim?"

Out of his trance Jim seemed quickly to wake, and he hugged his Della.

Jim drew a package from his overcoat pocket and threw it upon the table.

"Don't make any mistake, Dell," he said, "about me. I don't think there's anything in the way of a haircut or a shave or a shampoo that could make me like my girl any less.

"But if you'll unwrap that package, you may see why you had me going at first."

Nimble fingers tore at the string and paper. And then an ecstatic scream of joy; and then, alas! a quick change to hysterical tears and wails, prompting Jim to comfort Della.

For there lay The Combs—the set of combs, side and back, that Della had worshiped for so long in a Broadway window.

Beautiful combs, pure tortoise shell with jeweled rims—the perfect shade to wear in the beautiful vanished hair.

They were expensive combs, she knew, and her heart had simply craved and yearned over them without the least hope of possession. And now they were hers, but the tresses that should have adorned them were gone.

But she hugged them to her, and at length she was able to look up with dim eyes and a smile and say, "My hair grows so fast, Jim!"

And then Della leaped up like a little burned cat and cried, "Oh, oh!"

Jim had not yet seen his beautiful present. She held it out to him eagerly upon her open palm. The dull precious metal seemed to flash with a reflection of her bright and ardent spirit.

"Isn't it a dandy, Jim? I hunted all over town to find it. You'll have to look at the time a hundred times a day now. Give me your watch. I want to see how the chain looks on it."

Instead of obeying, Jim tumbled down on the couch and put his hands under the back of his head and smiled in an odd way.

"Dell," said he, "let's put our Christmas presents away and keep them awhile. They're too nice to use just now.

"I sold my watch to get the money to buy your combs. And now suppose you put the chops on."

The Magi, as you know, were wise men—
wonderfully wise men—who brought gifts to the
Babe in the manger. They invented the art of giving
Christmas presents. Being wise, their gifts were no
doubt wise ones. And here I have lamely related to
you the uneventful story of two foolish children in
an apartment who most unwisely sacrificed for each
other the greatest treasures of their house.

But in a last word to the wise of these days, let it
be said that of all who give gifts, these two were the
wisest, for theirs were the gifts of love.

Everywhere they are the wisest. They are the magi.